Ling

Maddy

Alphonse

Harry

Claudia

Vikram

Georgia

**For Edward, Clare,
Alexander and Anna**

First published 1999 by Walker Books Ltd
87 Vauxhall Walk, London SE11 5HJ

2 4 6 8 10 9 7 5 3 1

This book has been set in AT Arta Medium.

Printed in Hong Kong

British Library Cataloguing in Publication Data
A catalogue record for this book is
available from the British Library.

ISBN 0-7445-6161-2

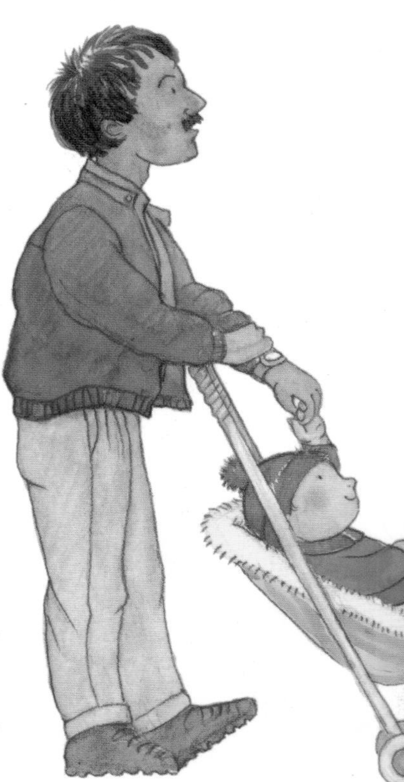

Toddlerobics
Animal Fun

Zita Newcome

WALKER BOOKS
AND SUBSIDIARIES
LONDON • BOSTON • SYDNEY

Give yourself a jiggle, come join in –

Animal Fun is about to begin!

Waddle like a penguin from side to side,

Flip your fins – imagine you're a fish!

back straight, arms down, feet out wide.

Swim through the sea with a splish, splash, splish!

Scuttle
like a crab
on your feet
and hands.

Thisaway,

thataway,

across

the sands.

Hands can be starfish –

stretch fingers wide.

Now floating jellyfish,

swirling in the tide.

Quack
like a duck
and
bend down low.

Move
your elbows
to and fro.

Squat
like a frog,
flick your
tongue in the sky.

Jump
right up and
catch that fly!

Roar!

You're a lion!

Snap!

You're a croc!

Be a kangaroo!
Go hop, hop, hop!

Swing your arms like a monkey in a tree.

Whoop and scratch and jump with glee!

Stomp like an elephant,

Circle round the room with a

lift that trunk.

thump, thump, thump!

Put hands together, make a hissing snake.

Gallop like a horse, give your mane a shake!

Flutter
your
wings –
be a
butterfly.

Swoop
down low,
then
soar up
high.

Lie on

your tummy,

wriggle like

a worm.

Roll and

writhe,

twist and

squirm.

Take deep
breaths
as you lie
on the ground.
Sssshh!
Curl up
and don't
make a sound.

That was GREAT!

Let's all take a bow.

Toddlerobics is fun

when you know how!

Ling
Maddy
Alphonse
Harry
Claudia
Vikram
Georgia
Archie